W9-BLQ-745

RAGGEDY ANN and ANDY
The Little Gray Kitten

by Polly Curren

illustrated by June Goldsborough

 GOLDEN PRESS
Western Publishing Company, Inc.
Racine, Wisconsin

© 1975 by The Bobbs-Merrill Company, Inc.
All rights reserved.
Produced in U.S.A. by Western Publishing Company, Inc.

Fourth Printing, 1978

All the dolls knew something special was going to happen. Raggedy Ann was dressed in a fresh white apron, and Andy was wearing a brand-new tie!

French Doll, China Doll, and all the others were wearing their best outfits. Soldier Doll stood stiff and tall, at attention.

When Marcella had dressed them that afternoon, she had been very excited. "Company's coming!" she had told them.

Now the Raggedys and the other dolls were in the garden, waiting. . . .

Raggedy Ann was the first one to see something interesting. "Here comes Next-door Lady," she whispered to Andy, "and she's carrying a basket."

"Marcella," Next-door Lady called. "Your company is here!"

Very gently, Next-door Lady lifted three small kittens from her basket and set them on the ground. The Raggedys and the other dolls smiled. They knew right away that the kittens were Mrs. Cat's new children.

One was white.

One was yellow.

And one was soft, smoky gray.

"Oh! Oh!" Marcella clapped her hands in delight.

"The white kitty is Snowball, the yellow one is Buttercup, and the gray one we call Kitten Little," Next-door Lady told Marcella. "I thought you might like to play with them while Mrs. Cat is taking a nap."

Marcella and the dolls were delighted!

What fun everyone had that afternoon! The kittens
did such funny things.

They ran around in circles, chasing their tails. Then
they chased each other. They even chased their bouncy
kitten-shadows!

Snowball and Buttercup climbed and tumbled all over each other.

Kitten Little went off to follow a long, wiggly worm to its hole in the ground.

All three kittens played ball with Marcella. Kitten Little chased the ball so fast that he kept falling over on his nose. Once he landed—*kerPLUNK*—right in the middle of the flower bed!

Marcella laughed and said, "You'd better rest here beside Raggedy Ann."

Kitten Little curled up comfortably, close to Raggedy Ann, who was as pleased as she could be.

But then, without any warning, it began to rain. Marcella's mother ran out to rescue the kittens.

Quickly scooping up all her dolls, Marcella piled them in the dolls' cradle. She carried them up to the nursery, where she left them in a jumbled heap.

Just as soon as the door closed, out of the heap jumped Kitten Little!

The dolls were delighted to have Kitten Little visiting them. Dutch Doll brought a cushion for him to sit on. Soldier Doll played a tune on his trumpet.

Then Fireman Doll took the kitten for a ride on his red fire engine.

Only Raggedy Ann was worried. Marcella might not visit the dolls again until morning. Raggedy Ann knew that Mrs. Cat soon would be looking for her little gray kitty.

The house grew dark and quiet.

Kitten Little was sleepy. "I want to go home now," he said.

Raggedy Ann fixed Dutch Doll's cushion into a cozy bed. "You can sleep here tonight," she said.

But the little gray kitten shook his head. "No—I want to go home," he said.

The dolls were upset. "What shall we do, Raggedy Ann?" they whispered.

"We must find some way to keep Kitten Little happy," Raggedy Ann told them.

French Doll spoke up. "He needs to play," she said.

So everybody played tag and hide-the-button until they were too tired to play any longer.

Kitten Little blinked his eyes and yawned three times. "I want to go home now," he said.

Baby Doll whispered, "He needs to eat. There's milk in my bottle. I'll give it to him."

Baby Doll poured the milk into a dish, and Kitten Little lapped up every drop.

"Now I want to go home," he said. "Please?" The little gray kitten looked so sad that the dolls were afraid he was going to cry.

"He needs to laugh," Clown Doll said quickly.

Clown Doll stood on his head. Then he made funny finger-shadows on the wall. Kitten Little laughed and laughed.

But as soon as Clown Doll stopped doing tricks, Kitten Little grew unhappy again.

"I want to go home *right now!*" he said.

Then Andy had an idea!

"I know what Kitten Little needs to make him happy," he said to Raggedy Ann. Then he whispered something in her ear.

Smiling, Raggedy Ann picked up Kitten Little and began to rock him. Two minutes later, the little gray kitten was sound asleep, safe in Raggedy Ann's soft cotton arms.

In the morning, Marcella and Mrs. Cat found him there.

"Here's Kitten Little!" Marcella cried in surprise. "Who would have thought we'd find him here with Raggedy Ann?"

"Meow," said Mrs. Cat, sounding very wise. She had been sure all along that her gray kitten was safe in the nursery.

Marcella praised her dolls for being so good to the little kitten. Then she hugged Raggedy Ann and Andy very tight. "The Raggedys always make everyone happy!" she said.

Raggedy Ann's and Andy's smiles grew one whole inch wider.

"We try to," the Raggedys' smiles seemed to say.